robbie the reindeer

HOOVES OF FIRE

Words by Glenn Dakin,
based on an award-winning
3-D model animation by Andy Riley,
Kevin Cecil and Richard Curtis

Illustrations by Delphine Thomas

COMIC
RELIEF

Our story begins in the north. North of Scotland.
North of where Björk lives. North of the Cold
Northlands, the Colder Northerlands and even
the coldest Northestlands.
It begins in Coldchester, the town at the North Pole.
Where, as you can probably tell, it is August . . .

And August is when the bus comes. This year, the bus has brought with it a small reindeer called Robbie, and this is his story. Robbie was a special reindeer. His nose knew the right way to go, even if he didn't. Using his suitcase as a sledge, Robbie whizzed through the snow – straight for Reindeer Lodge, home of Santa's sleigh team!

Robbie arrived, half-swallowed up
by his suitcase. At first, the other
reindeer didn't know what he was.
"It must be some rare and endangered species!"
gasped Donner, a kindly young girl reindeer.
"Cool. Let's kill it!" suggested Prancer,
a big, fat reindeer with an undersized brain.
Robbie introduced himself just in time.
"Call me Robbie," he said, "because I am."

A tall reindeer strode forward and shook Robbie by the hoof.

"I'm Blitzen, the leader of the sleigh team," he smiled. "Any problems, come and see me. If you don't have any problems, see me anyway, and we'll celebrate your lack of problems!"

Robbie was sure they were going to be great friends.

"So you've come to join the team," Blitzen beamed.

"Yeah," Robbie replied. "I've come to steer the sleigh!"

Robbie could find his way anywhere with his nose. The other reindeer named any place on the globe, and, as if it had a life of its own, Robbie's nose pointed straight to it. Amazing!

"This is going to be a huge laugh," Robbie said. "Just one thing. I know what we'll be doing for ONE day of the year – but what do we do for the other three hundred and sixty-four?"

Blitzen grinned. "For this one sleigh ride, we work out every single day!"

"What? No partying? No strumming guitars around the log fire?"

"Sorry, Robbie . . . " Blitzen said sadly.

"Right," Robbie replied. "When's the next bus out?"

There was no bus out until next year.

"If you're not into exercise, why are you here?" Donner asked.

"My dad sent me," explained Robbie. "Character building. Apparently I'm easily distracted."

"She's nice, isn't she?" he whispered.

"That's Vixen," said Donner, quickly showing Robbie to his tiny room.

Meanwhile, Blitzen was holding a meeting with the senior members of the team.

"Robbie's new around here, and he might find it hard to settle in. I'd like you to help me – make his life a misery! Destroy him! Throw what's left to the wolves – then blow up the wolves!"

"This is about his dad, isn't it?" Vixen asked.

"I hate his dad!" raged Blitzen. "He was always the favourite! I will not sleep until I've destroyed Robbie!"

That night there was a special get-together at Santa's house. The old man threw the coolest parties. Soon, the evening was in full swing. The reindeer were getting down, and Seal was singing his greatest hits. Well, *a* seal was. Everyone was having a groovy time. Except Vixen.

"Well, this is a room with some animals in it," she said witheringly. Then she slunk over to Robbie. "I was sent some flowers today," she said coldly. "I knew they were from you . . . because they were CHEAP!" she snorted. Robbie felt totally miserable.

Santa showed them an amazing new sleigh he had designed.

"It has an automatic navigation system, so we won't need anyone to steer it!" Robbie was horrified. "But that doesn't mean Robbie isn't coming," Santa continued hastily. "Blitzen has come up with a fair way of deciding who stays behind. It will be the reindeer who is the least fit!" Robbie knew who that was . . . him! He left the party sadly. All his hopes were in ruins.

Back at the lodge, Blitzen pretended to feel sorry for Robbie.

"Cheer up," he said. "Santa will probably take you anyway. The sleigh will be slow and late, and little children will wake up on Christmas morning, and get nothing!"

Robbie felt terrible. He walked to the door, his head bowed low, and trudged off into the snowy night.

Robbie was only a small, lazy, easily distracted reindeer, and he didn't last long
all alone out in the snow. Soon, he was frozen into a great block of ice.
Eventually, some passing elves found him, dragged him back home and popped
him on the barbecue.

"Do it till it's crispy!" said one elf. "I like the crispy bits!"

"Hope there's leftovers – we can make a curry!" suggested another. But they
were both disappointed – Robbie simply thawed out and came back to life. The
elves didn't have the heart to eat him – in fact, the Head Elf let him have a job
in their toy factory.

At first, Robbie made himself useful. Then he fell into one of the toy-making machines and was boxed up as a talking doll.

The elves decided he should sweep up instead. Robbie soon got bored of this, and started inventing some new toys of his own.

"Look," Robbie grinned. "Sebastian Musclewhale!" But the Head Elf was not impressed. Neither did he think much of Sebastian's arch-enemy, Octo-Monkey. Soon Robbie was demoted again.

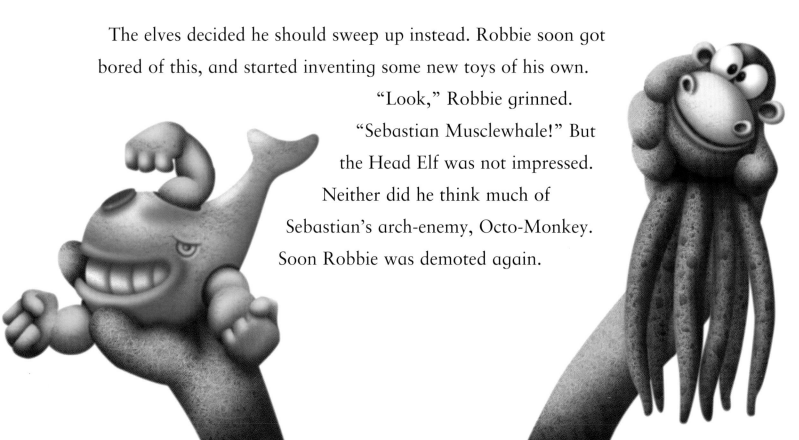

One day, Donner came to the factory to pick up an order of gym equipment.
There she was astonished to discover Robbie tied to the front of a fork-lift truck!

It wasn't long before poor Robbie was pouring out his woes to her, as they huddled together outside.

"I was a rubbish deer," said Robbie. "I'm even a rubbish elf!" But Donner had an idea for how Robbie could earn himself a place on Santa's sleigh team.

"Just before Christmas, there's a big sports tournament called the Reindeer Races. If you go all out to win a medal, you could get your place back!"

Robbie decided it was worth a try.

"I'll do it!" he said proudly. "For me. For my dad. And most of all . . . for Vixen!"

"Yeah. Beautiful Vixen," Donner groaned.

"You can't work out with the other reindeer," Donner said. "Blitzen'll do anything to stop you winning."

"But he's my best friend!" protested Robbie.

Donner gave Robbie some binoculars so he could see into Blitzen's room. Through the window he saw a nice big picture of himself – being bombarded by darts! Then knives. Then a meat cleaver. They were all being thrown by Blitzen.

"Some friend he is. I say we whop him good!" Robbie said.

"We'll need help," Donner replied. "I looked in the phone book under "Wise Old Coaches Who Can Save The Day" and there was only one in the area. His name's Old Jingle!"

At the top of Pointy Mountain – the highest peak at the North Pole – stood the house of Old Jingle. It creaked backwards and forwards in the howling wind, ready to fall off and slide down the mountain at any moment.

An old reindeer with a mad look in his eye opened the door.

"Is Old Jingle in?" asked Robbie.

"Let me think . . . " pondered the old figure, as if it were a very tough question. "Yes, I am! Come in, I'll put the kettle on." So he put the kettle on his head.

"I want you to train me for the Reindeer Races, sir," Robbie said.

Suddenly, Old Jingle leapt to his feet.

"Well, Robbiepupil, let's get down the hill and I'll see what you're made of."

As they all got up to leave together, the house suddenly overbalanced and slid all the way down the mountain.

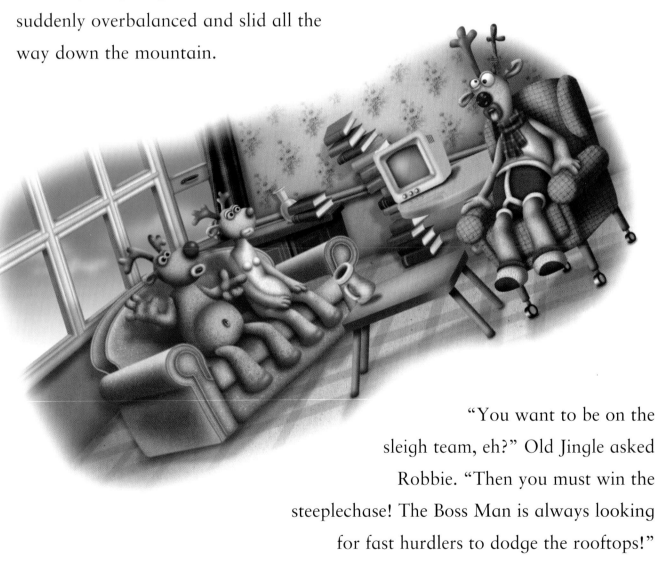

"You want to be on the sleigh team, eh?" Old Jingle asked Robbie. "Then you must win the steeplechase! The Boss Man is always looking for fast hurdlers to dodge the rooftops!"

From then on, Old Jingle worked for hours,
days, weeks, getting Robbie into shape.
One day, he took Robbie for some
very special training.
He tied his legs together and
told him to jump over a hurdle.
"I can't!" Robbie cried out.
"Yes, you can," said Old Jingle, speaking
in a mysterious way. "If you use your
NOSE! Bounce with your nose!" he
commanded. "Trust your nose!"
Finally, a day came when Robbie could
do nose press-ups and bounce right
over the hurdles, just using his nose!
Everyone congratulated him – Robbie
was finally ready for the Races!

And so, Robbie set off for the greatest challenge of his life.

When he and Donner left, Old Jingle looked around at the place where his home had come to rest in the snow.

"Nice spot for a house," he said. "I'd have to be crazy to push my place back up Pointy Mountain!"

And so, of course, he did. Suddenly . . .

"AARGH!" The house slipped back on top of him.

Unknown to Robbie, his friend had just been flattened.

The North Pole Stadium
was packed with cheering deer.
 "Welcome to the Reindeer Races,"
announced Des Yeti, who was with his expert
assistant, Alan Snowman. Santa and Mrs
Santa were there, too. Des Yeti announced the
arrival of the great singing attraction . . . the
three ten-tonners! These were colossal walruses
who sang great operatic showstoppers –
if someone would just throw them a few fish.

"So, on with the Races!" Des Yeti declared. "The question everyone's asking is: 'Which Reindeer will be the star?'"

One reindeer was determined to make sure it was him no matter what he had to do. In a dark changing room, Blitzen swallowed his wicked potion in secret. Suddenly, he was much stronger. In moments, he was out on the track astonishing the crowd with his speed and skill.

"Blitzen hasn't lost an event yet!" said Des Yeti. "But the most important one is still to come – the steeplechase."

"And we've got a late entrant. Who's this? Seems to be a young reindeer we haven't seen before." It was Robbie!

"Why is he here?" Blitzen asked furiously. Vixen sighed.

"Don't worry about him. Everyone's here to see you. Wave to them!"

Everyone waved back, including the three ten-tonners. Then – disaster – one of the walruses slapped one of his chums on the back, and he was sent plummeting to the ground below. He was heading straight for Baby Santa who was sitting helplessly at the bottom.

A hush fell on the stadium. Only one reindeer was brave enough – and fast enough – to race to the rescue . . . Robbie! He leapt over the side of the track and snatched the baby to safety just before the walrus hit the ground and pancaked out.

The crowd went wild. Donner hugged Robbie. Blitzen was aghast.

What had turned Robbie into a hero? Vixen took control of the situation.

"Look Robbie, you love me. You'll do anything for me," she cooed. "I don't want you to run. I want Blitzen to win so he gets famous and takes me out of this dive!"

"Sorry, Vixen, but I'm going to try to win," said Robbie. Vixen couldn't believe her ears.

"Robbie! You spoke to me! I thought you couldn't talk to girls you loved."

"I grew up," Robbie said. Donner asked Robbie if he was all set for the race, but now Robbie found he couldn't talk to her!

Suddenly, the Head Elf came speeding up on his snowmobile.

"Robbie! Old Jingle's trapped under his house! I can't lift it!"

Just then, all runners were asked to report for the start of the steeplechase. What was Robbie going to do?

He realised he had to go and sped off.

"The little reindeer's actually running out of the stadium!" Des Yeti commentated.

"You never win a race that way, Des," said Alan Snowman. "That's inexperience."

Robbie found Old Jingle, squashed beneath his house.

"I need something to wedge underneath!" Robbie said.

The Head Elf found . . . Sebastian Musclewhale! Then he produced Octo-Monkey. With the two toys holding up the house, Robbie eventually managed to pull his trainer to safety.

"Sebastian and Octo-Monkey," said Robbie proudly. "They joined forces for the first time!" Old Jingle looked up at Robbie weakly.

"Farewell . . . Robbiefriend!" he croaked. His eyes closed.

"Jingle!" Robbie wailed. The old reindeer woke up with a snort.

"Can't I have a nap?" he asked. "Now when does this race start?"

From far away, they heard the crack of the starting pistol. The race had begun.

"Well? *Run!*" ordered Old Jingle. By the time Robbie got there, he was three laps behind Blitzen. He raced like he had never raced before, and soon the lead was down to two laps . . . then one! Donner was cheering wildly.

"Blitzen and Robbie are neck and neck!" said Des Yeti.

But Blitzen wasn't interested in running a fair race. He swung the final hurdle round to smash Robbie to the floor. Tired and hurt, Robbie could see no way he was going to get over that hurdle. From far away he seemed to hear Old Jingle call to him.

"The nose jump, Robbie! Use the nose jump!"

Blitzen took the final hurdle, sure that victory was his. Then, to his utter amazement, he saw Robbie flying through the air towards him. They both headed for the finishing line, side by side. It was a photo finish. There was a hush as everyone waited for the picture to develop.

The elf judge looked closely at the print. "The winner – by a nose – is Blitzen!" There was a huge groan of disappointment. Blitzen punched the air in celebration. "Yeeeessss!" he cried.

Robbie collapsed, and Donner rushed to his side.

"Robbie. I'm proud of you!" Donner said. Then she kissed him. Suddenly, Robbie sprang to life. He raced around the track like lightning. He hurled the javelin so fast it melted. He leapt the pole vault twice as high as Blitzen ever had.

"Incredibly, Robbie is now beating all the records for every event!" Des Yeti gasped.

The crowds cheered wildly. Blitzen was furious. Soon, the judges appeared before him. They knew Blitzen had taken his wicked potion before the events, and declared that he was nothing but a cheat. As he was dragged away, Vixen called after him.

"By the way – you're chucked!"
Santa congratulated Robbie.

"Ever led a sleigh before?" he asked. "You'll need to get some practice in, now you're on the team. Here – it's yours for the night!"

Robbie flew Santa's new sleigh all the way to the Moon,
where he and Donner sat together in the romantic earthlight.
And they all lived happily ever after – except Vixen, who was
last seen hitch-hiking away from the North Pole. And Blitzen,
who ended up with a job that he truly deserved – making
brand new toys for next Christmas . . .
models of Robbie!

The End